6

THE BACKPACK AQUARIUM

Written & illustrated by

MICHAEL REX

A STEPPING STONE BOOK™

Random House 🏠 New York

To Simon and Richard, for their vision . . .

Visit us on the Web!
SteppingStonesBooks.com
randomhousekids.com

Educators and librarians, for a variety of teaching tools,
visit us at RHTeachersLibrarians.com

Library of Congress Cataloging-in-Publication Data
Rex, Michael, author, illustrator.
The backpack aquarium / written & illustrated by Michael Rex.
p. cm. — (Icky Ricky ; 6)
"A Stepping Stone Book"
Summary: "Icky Ricky gets into plenty of trouble, including fish swimming in his backpack,
wearing a disguise made out of trash, and playing soccer with a snake in his pocket."
—Provided by publisher.
ISBN 978-0-385-37562-7 (trade) — ISBN 978-0-385-37563-4 (lib. bdg.) —
ISBN 978-0-385-37564-1 (ebook)
[1. Humorous stories. 2. Behavior—Fiction.] I. Title.
PZ7.R32875Bac 2015 [E]—dc23 2015008227

Printed in the United States of America
10 9 8 7 6 5 4 3 2 1

This book has been officially leveled by the F&P Text Level Gradient™ Leveling System.

CONTENTS

"Ricky!" cried Ricky's mom as he ran straight into her on the sidewalk. "Why are you covered in white powder, and why is there a box on your head?"

"Because I couldn't live forever in a Dumpster!" said Ricky.

Ricky's mom crossed her arms and
then gave Ricky her best mom stare. He
could never resist the mom stare. He
had to slow down and start the story
from the beginning. Ricky took a deep
breath. . . .

It all started when you asked me and Gus and Stew to walk down to the post office and mail your letter while you went to the grocery store. At the post office, we were looking for the right slot to put the letter in when we saw something excellent!

There were these really cool "Wanted" posters on the wall. I'd never seen real "Wanted" posters. I thought that they only existed in cowboy movies. We started reading the crimes that the guys were wanted for.

"This one says 'Breaking and Entering,'" said Gus.

"I wonder what he broke," said Stew.

"I wonder what he entered," I said.

"Maybe he snuck into a supermarket and broke all the eggs!" said Gus.

We all studied the Breaking and Entering guy's face closely. He was kind of scary-looking. Stew pointed at another poster.

"This guy's wanted for 'Grand Larceny,'" said Gus.

"What's that?" asked Stew.

"I think he stole one thousand dollars," I said. "Crooks call one thousand dollars a grand."

"That's a lot of money," said Gus. "I wouldn't even know what to do with that much money."

"But you'd have to hide it so that this guy wouldn't steal it," said Stew.

"I know how I'd hide my money!"
I said. "I'd get a little box and write 'My
Best Boogers Ever' on it and put the money
in there. No one would ever open that."

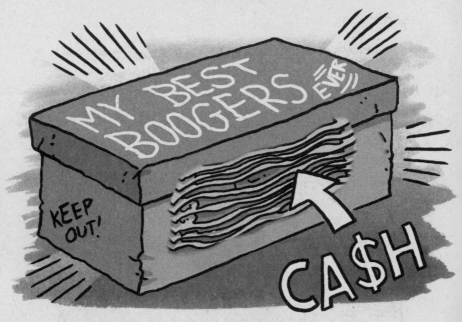

"But where would you put your
boogers?" asked Stew.

"Duh. They go in my pocket," I said.

We stared at the picture of the Grand
Larceny guy. He was kind of scary, too.

"This one did 'Fraud' and 'Disturbing
the Peace,'" said Gus, pointing at the last
poster.

"What's fraud?" I asked.

"It's like when you fake someone out," said Gus. "Like if you sell someone a painting for a million dollars and say that it was painted by Picasso, but it was really painted by your baby brother at day care."

"I wonder what disturbing the peace is,"
I said. "That sounds like almost anything."

"Yeah, like shooting off fireworks," said
Gus.

"Or driving a hot rod around late at
night," said Stew.

"Or shooting off fireworks from the
back of a hot rod and screaming 'YOLO!'"
I said.

We all started laughing. The post office workers glared at us.

We inspected the picture of the last guy and saw that he was scary, too. It seemed that to be a crook, you had to look mean and tough.

"I wonder if any of these guys are around here," said Gus.

That's when I had my best idea of the day.

"We should go searching for these guys and turn them in to the police!" I said.

We each chose one crook and memorized his face. We remembered the way the guys had their hair cut and if they had scars or beards or eye patches or anything. None of them had eye patches, but you know what I mean.

We left the post office and tried to
figure out where to hunt first.

"If we go that way," I said as I pointed
away from the post office, "it's just back
to houses, but the other way goes down to
stores and stuff."

"There're some alleys, too," said Gus.
"Crooks always hang out in alleys."

We walked off toward the center of town, where all the shops and alleys were. Every time we saw a man, we checked him out closely to see if he was one of the criminals.

We were staring at this one guy and he glared at us and was like, "Can I help you?"

"No," we said.

He seemed kind of annoyed.

We didn't see anyone who looked scary or like they could commit a crime. Just some moms, some old people, and a few men who weren't the crooks.

Then I peeked into the little shoe store. There was a man in there, and he was helping a lady and her kids.

"Hey! You see that guy?" I said.

We all pressed our faces up to the glass.

"He looks like Breaking and Entering Guy," I said.

"Except his hair is dark. The guy in the picture had light hair," said Stew.

"Maybe he dyed it," said Gus.

"Yeah!" I said. "He's in disguise!"

Just then, the man saw us. He seemed angry.

We ran from the shop and down the street. We hid behind a garbage can. We looked down the street, and he was coming toward us! We could hear him shouting.

"Follow me!" I shouted to Stew and Gus. We ran into the hardware store. Once inside, we walked quickly through the aisles.

"Why are we here?" asked Gus.

"We have to lose him," I said. We ran to the rear of the store and out the back door.

We snuck down a skinny alley and out onto the sidewalk again. We couldn't see him anywhere.

"We lost him," said Gus.

"Hey, kids!" we heard a man yell. "Come here!"

We spun around and ran into the alley.
We saw a big Dumpster and jumped into it.
We closed the lid and hid from Breaking
and Entering Guy.

"What are we going to do?" asked Gus.

"We can stay here," I said.

"How long?" asked Gus.

"As long as we need to. Maybe forever,"
I said.

"I bet we could live here if we needed
to," said Stew.

We dug through the stuff in the Dumpster. Even though it was behind the hardware store, there wasn't anything really good in it. There were a bunch of cardboard boxes, a few pieces of wood, a broken shovel, and some big ripped bags of plaster powder.

"I don't know how long we'd last here. There's no food and no water," I said. "One of us is going to have to go for help."

The guys agreed.

"Since I was the one who suggested we look for bad guys, I'll go for help," I said. "I'll find my mom or a cop."

"You need a disguise," said Stew.

"Yeah," said Gus. "That way Breaking and Entering Guy won't know that it's you."

"Excellent idea!" I said. "Let's switch shirts, Stew! That will confuse him."

Stew and I took our shirts off and traded them. Gus took off his sneakers, and I gave him mine. I looked like a totally different kid. But my hair was still the same.

"What are we going to do about your hair?" asked Gus.

Searching around the Dumpster, we noticed we were getting covered with the white plaster powder.

"What about this?" said Gus. He took a big handful of the powder and started rubbing it in my hair. It got all caked in my curls and was clumpy, but soon it made my hair look just about white.

"Ta-da!" said Stew. "You're a really old kid."

"Or a really short old man," said Gus.

"Yeah!" I said. "I'll be an old man, and Breaking and Entering Guy won't even recognize me! I could walk right past him!"

I pulled my pants up really high and tucked my shirt into them. Stew grabbed a small, flat box and put it on my head. "Here, use this as a hat."

"It doesn't really look like a hat," said Gus.

"Yeah, but maybe the old guy lost his glasses, and he put this box on his head and thinks it's a hat," said Stew.

"Old people can get away with being really strange and no one cares," said Gus. He handed me the busted shovel.

"A cane!" I said. "Perfect." I was ready to go get help.

We opened the Dumpster just a tiny bit. We were alone in the alley.

As I climbed out of the Dumpster, it occurred to me that I might never see Gus and Stew again.

"Gus," I said, "if I don't come back, you can have all my sports stuff. Even the string from the baseball that I unwound."

"Thanks," said Gus.

"Stew, you can have all my art and building stuff. Including the five-gallon bucket of black paint that's hidden in my parents' closet."

"Thanks," said Stew.

"What about all of your experiments?" asked Gus.

"I want you to make sure they go to a scientist or some sort of a museum," I said. "The world needs to know how long a tomato wrapped in a scarf can last between two mattresses."

"Sure," said Gus and Stew.

"It's been an honor serving with you!" I said, and I gave Gus and Stew a military salute.

They both saluted back and said, "Yessir! You too, sir!"

I pulled my pants up even higher, leaned on the stick, and slowly walked out of the alley. I was kind of nervous, so I started running.

"Old guys can't run!" shouted Gus from the Dumpster.

That's when I came out of the alley and bumped into you.

"I see," said Ricky's mom.

"Excuse me," said a voice. Ricky and his mom both turned around. It was Breaking and Entering Guy.

"Hi, Jack!" said Ricky's mom.

"Hello, Teresa," said Jack. "How are you?"

"I'm fine, thanks. How about you?" asked Ricky's mom.

"Well, I was having a pretty good day," he said. "Until I had to chase this kid and his friends all over town." He looked at Ricky.

Ricky was frozen with fear.

Ricky stared at the man's face carefully. He wasn't scary-looking at all. Ricky had the wrong guy.

"For some reason," said Jack, "you and your friends were leaning on my store window, getting it smudged up. It will take me all afternoon to clean it."

"S-s-s-sorry," said Ricky. "How did you recognize me in my old man disguise?"

Ricky's mom and Jack laughed.

"Then when you ran away, you dropped this," said Jack. "I've been trying to give it back to you." He held up the letter Ricky had promised to mail for his mom.

"Ricky!" said his mom. "I told you to mail this."

"Well," said Ricky, "I guess I've gotten a little forgetful in my old age!"

ICKY RICKY'S

DREAM JOBS

(Part 1)

Adults always ask kids what they want to be when they grow up. Most of them say stuff like doctor, teacher, or fireman.
I don't want to be any of those. I've got my own list of what I call "dream jobs"!

Tire Factory Tire Bouncer

Nacho Inspector

Private Stench Investigator

"Ricky!" said Coach Ron as he quickly tapped Ricky's shin to make sure he was wearing shin guards. "Why the heck are you so late?"

"Because Dr. Fangenstein was deejaying an awesome party!" said Ricky.

"I can't even begin to figure out what that means," said Coach Ron. He looked closely at Ricky's right foot. "What's this goop coming out of your cleat?"

"It's glue!" said Ricky.

"Why is your cleat glued on?" asked the coach. "Did Dr. Whatever-stein do that, too?"

"Of course not!" said Ricky. "I did! Let me explain. . . ."

It all started this morning.

I went out to my backyard looking for something, but when I got out there, I couldn't remember what I needed to find. I started goofing around and digging under a bush, looking for some worms or something, and I found a little green snake!

It was really friendly and didn't mind me holding it. First I let it slip through my fingers, then I let it crawl on my arms.

I got down on my back and let it wiggle all
over my stomach. It went in the neck of
my shirt and came out the sleeve. It even
crawled through my hair. It was really cool.

I wanted to find a place for it to live.
I looked around in my garage. I found a
few cardboard boxes, but they all had holes
that he could escape out of. Then I found
something excellent.

It was an old glass aquarium that we
used to keep fish in. It was perfect for a
snake. It was empty except for a statue of a
scuba diver guy in a shark cage.

I filled the aquarium with some dirt, leaves, grass, and rocks, and I put the shark cage guy back in. The little snake crawled right up on top of the cage and hung out there. It looked like he had caught the guy and put him in a jail. He seemed kind of evil, but I knew he was nice.

I decided to name the snake Dr. Fangenstein, even though he didn't have fangs. I had a really cool idea to make a super-villain's lair for him. That's when I remembered that I had come outside looking for something. But I still couldn't remember what. I searched around the garage. Whatever it was, it wasn't there.

I found a box of old, broken toys from when I was a little kid. First, I put a toy car in the villain's lair so Dr. Fangenstein would have a getaway car if the good guys ever found him. Next, I jammed an old squirt gun into the dirt so it was pointing at the sky like some sort of death ray. Every super-villain needs a death ray.

I tried to make him a little computer with some other junk. I put two bottle caps on a little block of wood. It didn't look at all like a computer. But it did look like a totally cool turntable! I picked up Dr. Fangenstein and draped him over the turntable. His tail swooshed across one of the bottle caps, and it looked like he was at an excellent party, scratchin' records.

I looked in the garage again to see
if there was anything else I could use in
the lair. I moved a skateboard and found
my soccer cleats. *That's* what I had been
looking for.

SOCCER!

I totally forgot! It was Saturday morning, and I have soccer games on Saturday mornings.

I grabbed the cleats and ran up to my room as fast as possible. I found my soccer uniform. It was still in a ball at the foot of my bed from last week. Just where it was supposed to be. I put on the shirt, shorts, and socks.

I found the shin guards and shoved them in my socks. I put my first cleat on and laced it up. I grabbed the second one, but the lace was gone.

Duh! During the week I had made a
survival kit for my bike. I had put a bottle
of water, a piece of fried chicken, a cleanish
pair of underwear, a harmonica, a hockey
puck, three rubber bands, a button, and a
plastic army man with no head into a bag.
I had used the lace from my cleat to tie the
bag closed and hang it on my bike. That
way if I ever got lost, I'd have all that stuff
to survive.

I thought about getting the lace from the survival kit, but I knew it would be knotted up too tight. I frantically searched my room for something to use as a lace. I yanked a string from a yo-yo and tried that. It snapped in half when I tried to tie it.

I took a string from the neck of a sweatshirt, but it was too thick to go in the holes on the cleat. I took apart a little bracelet I had made in arts and crafts, but that string was all stretchy and wouldn't hold the shoe on tight.

I picked up a roll of tape and yanked off the last piece. I tried to wrap it around my cleat, but it was too short!

Then I had my best idea of the day. I grabbed a bottle of glue, poured it into the shoe, and stuck my foot in. It was just sticky enough so that my foot didn't slip out.

I got on my bike and rode to the soccer field as fast as I could. I was really thirsty when I got there. I tried to get the water bottle from the survival kit. Yup! I was right! I had tied it way too tight and couldn't open it. I gave up on that, and I ran over to you!

Coach Ron just shook his head.

"I'm sorry I asked," he said. "The game's about to start. You think that cleat will stay on?"

"Sure," said Ricky.

"Then get on out there," said Coach Ron as he gave Ricky a quick tap on the back.

Ricky took his position, and the referee
blew the whistle to start the game. Ricky's
team had the ball. Stew passed the ball to
Ricky, and he took off.

Ricky slipped past a few defenders. He
kicked the ball as hard as he could. The
ball went sailing toward the goal.

His shoe went flying into the air.
The ball shot over the goalie's hands.

Ricky's shoe landed on the ref's head.

DONK!

The team started screaming,
"Gooooooooallllllll!" But then the ref blew
the whistle and said, "No goal." Everyone
looked around, trying to figure out what
was going on.

Coach Ron and the ref ran over to
Ricky. "No goal," said the ref again.

"What do you mean, no goal?" asked
Coach Ron.

"It was a dangerous play," said the ref.

"How was it a dangerous play?" asked
Coach Ron.

"His shoe hit me in the head!" said the ref.

"Sorry my shoe hit you on the head, Ref," Ricky said.

The ref looked at Ricky and told him that he was fine, but the goal wouldn't count. Then the ref screamed, "Snake!"

Then Coach Ron screamed, "Snake!"
All the kids on both teams started
running all over the place, shouting,
"Snake! Snake!" Kids climbed the sides
of the goal. Kids jumped on each other's
shoulders. Even the moms and dads on the
sidelines were screaming, "Snake!"

"What the heck is going on?" said a man as he leaned out the window of his car. He was looking up at Ricky, who was hanging halfway out a school bus window. "Give me one good reason why you are hitting my car with a belt!" demanded the man.

"Because Michelle couldn't move her assigned seat!" said Ricky.

"Kid," said the man, "you're lucky we're stuck in traffic, because I'm not going anywhere until you explain yourself."

"All right," said Ricky. "This is what happened. . . ."

It all started on our field trip to the natural history museum. To get there, we had to take the George Washington Bridge.

There was tons of traffic, and the bus was hardly moving. Stew and I tried to look out the bus windows to see how high we were, but we were in a center lane and just saw lots of cars on either side.

"I wonder if this bridge is high enough so that you could jump off and still have time to open a parachute," I said.

"I don't know," said Stew. "A wing suit might be a better idea."

"Yeah, because then you could just fly down the river and go wherever you wanted," I said.

"Ugh!" said Michelle, who was sitting behind us. "Will you guys stop talking about jumping off the bridge?"

"Why?" I asked.

"I hate heights," she said. "They make me sick."

"Yeah, but we're in a bus in the middle of the road. Nothing's going to happen to us," I said.

The traffic started to move again, and there was lots of honking and stuff. The bus pulled over to the outside lane.

"Look, Stew," I said. "Check out how high we are."

Stew leaned over me and pressed his face against the window.

"Wow! We're like five hundred feet up!" said Stew.

We both tried to get a better view out the window. I opened it, and I stuck my head out. The bus was so close to the edge that we could almost see straight down.

"Stop, Ricky!" yelled Michelle. "You're freaking me out!"

I pulled my head in from the window. "Sorry," I said. She looked really nervous now.

"Why don't you change seats so you're on the other side of the bus?" I asked.

"You know we have assigned seats!" she said.

"She'll get in trouble if she moves," said Lisa, who was sitting next to her.

The bus inched forward a bit. I didn't think it was possible, but we got closer to the edge.

Michelle covered her eyes. "How long is this trip going to take?" she asked. Then she started to cry. Just a little, but I could see it. She was shaking, too.

"Let's play a game," I said. "It will distract you."

"No," she said. "Just leave me alone."

"C'mon! Let's play Garbage Mouth!" I said.

"Eww, no!" she said. "That's for little kids."

"What's Garbage Mouth?" asked Lisa.

Michelle rolled her eyes and said, "It's this dumb game where—"

I cut her off. "It's an awesome game where I'll eat anything that people give me. If I refuse, the other person wins."

"Sounds stupid," said Lisa.

"It is," said Michelle. "We played it every day in second-grade lunch."

"You used to love it!" I said.

"That's because I was a dumb second grader," she said.

Stew turned around and told the people in the seat in front of ours that we were going to play Garbage Mouth. We kept it quiet because our teacher is really strict on the bus. Some kids didn't know the game, but Stew explained it, and soon everyone was in on it.

All the kids on the bus opened their
lunches and looked for things for me to
eat. They started handing stuff to us. First
was a banana that had gotten black in
someone's lunch bag. I ate that in a second.

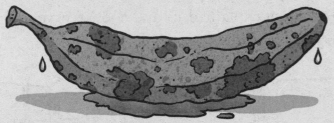

Then came half a peanut butter and
jelly sandwich that someone had put a slice
of cheese on. No problem.

Then came a bag of crushed tortilla chips that someone had poured applesauce and vanilla pudding in.

"Yummy!" I said as I licked my lips and rubbed my belly. Then stuff was coming fast, and I could barely keep up.

"Egg salad mixed in hummus with cheese balls? No problem," I said.

"Gummy worms wrapped in salami, with crushed chocolate chip cookies squished up with tofu? Awesome!" I said. "What's next?"

"White rice with a chewable multivitamin?" I asked. "You guys aren't even trying!"

"A leaf from someone's shoe? Mother Nature's own snack." I chomped down.

A group of kids put tuna fish salad, a cold chicken nugget, some raspberries, some whole wheat crackers, a piece of gluten-free chocolate, some lo mein, and a pretzel into a small container, smushed up with a spoon.

"I love it!" I said as I dug in.

Someone handed me a sock with something in it.

"That's against the rules," I said. "It has to be something I can digest."

"Open the sock!" someone said. I looked at the sock and knew that I had to eat whatever was inside it.

TO BE CONTINUED . . .

ICKY RICKY'S

DREAM JOBS

(Part 2)

I can't wait to grow up and get a job.
No matter what I choose, I am going to
be the best in the world at it!

Weasel Repairman

HERE YOU GO, MA'AM. GOOD AS NEW!

Fudge Judge

I DECLARE THIS FUDGE GUILTY! GUILTY OF BEING DELICIOUS!

Short-Order Pigs-in-a-Blanket Chef

The President of Mud

RRRRRR!

GRRRR!

"Ricky and Gus!" shouted Scoutmaster
Dave. "What are you doing down here
at the lake? And why is your backpack
glowing, Ricky?"

"Because I really like worms!" Ricky
told him as he and Gus stood up on the
dock.

"Ricky," said Scoutmaster Dave, "not
only does a scout always have to tell the
truth, but a scout also has to make sense.
Now just start at the beginning."

"Yes, sir!" said Ricky. . . .

It all started when we were fishing this afternoon. The older scouts taught us how to bait the hook with a worm, cast off, and reel in when we needed to start again. I didn't really like the idea of using a worm to catch a fish. I like worms, and I think it's cool how they can crawl right into the earth and that they make the dirt better for growing stuff.

But we had to catch fish for our badge. I took part of my lunch sandwich, ripped it into small pieces, and dropped the bread crumbs in the water. Gus found a net, and we got on our bellies with our hands hanging off the dock.

"Hahaha! That's never gonna work,"
said Dawson, who was in charge.

"You guys are a bunch of babies using
a net like that," said another kid. "You
should learn to fish the real way."

"Well, I don't want to hurt any worms,"
I said. "They never did anything to me!"

The older scouts laughed and laughed.

Gus and I ignored them. While they
were laughing, some fish swam to the top
and nibbled at the bread. I scooped them
up with the net. I got one and put it in a
bucket of water we had on the dock.

"Awesome," said Gus. Then he took
the net and had his turn. He scooped up a
fish, too. He put his in the bucket. We kept
doing this until the bread ran out.

Some of the older scouts who were
using worms hadn't even caught anything
yet.

"Hey, Dawson," I said. "Our bucket's
full. Can we throw the fish back now?"

"What?" said Dawson. "No, you don't throw them back. We bring them to camp and eat them for dinner."

"Really?" I said.

"What's the matter?" said Dawson. "Don't ya like fish?"

I told them I liked fish, but I didn't want to kill anything. "Can't we get our badges from this bucketful?" I asked.

"No," said Dawson. "I'll tell the scoutmaster that you threw them back, and you won't get your badge, and your whole afternoon will be wasted." He laughed.

"All right," I said. "We'll take them back to camp and eat them."

Gus looked at me like I was crazy. I winked at him.

"Yeah!" said Gus. "We're gonna fry these babies up and have a fish feast!"

"Mmmmmmm," I said, rubbing my stomach. "I'm gonna pull the bones out, roll them up, and make fish sticks!"

The older kids were all laughing now. We took the bucket and headed back in the direction of the camp. Once we were far enough from the water and the older boys, I turned away from camp and headed in a different direction.

"Where are we going?" asked Gus.

"We're gonna throw these guys back.
I don't want to eat them," I said.

"Yeah," said Gus. "I don't even like fish-
flavored potato chips."

We quietly walked through the woods
and then went back down to the lake.

"What about our fishing badges?"
asked Gus.

"Badge, shmadge," I said.

We were far away from the docks now.
We were about to dump the fish back in
the lake, when we heard a voice.

"Ricky! Gus! What are you two doing?" someone called. There were a group of scouts in canoes on the lake.

"Nothing!" I yelled. "Just looking around."

We couldn't dump the fish back in the water now! The scouts would see us and tell everyone else. We turned and walked back through the woods to the camp.

The water in the bucket seemed to be getting lower. We stopped and looked it over. It had a tiny hole in the bottom and it was leaking.

"What are we gonna do with all of these fish?" I asked.

"They gotta get back in the water," said Gus.

"I don't want them to die," I said. "Yikes! Let's get going!"

We got to our tent without anyone seeing us. We brought the bucket inside and zipped up the front of the tent. The water was really low. I looked around for something else to put the fish in.

We had a big, strong plastic bag that we hung our food in at night so animals wouldn't get it. I dumped out the food, and we poured the water and fish into the bag. Some of the water missed and went all over our camping stuff. Our tent was on a slight hill, and it all ran down into the corner. The sleeping bags and our clothes got soaked. Some bread and crackers got wet, too.

We were worried that the plastic
bag was going to rip, so we put it in my
backpack and piled up our sleeping bags
around it so it wouldn't tip.

We poured some more water in from
our water bottles. The fish seemed pretty
happy now. We put some crackers in, and
the fish ate them.

My backpack had a rip on one side,
so you could see the fish swimming at the
bottom.

"It's like an aquarium," I said.

"Yeah," said Gus. "Should we put some
more stuff in there? Like some colored
rocks or a toy sunken ship?"

"We don't have either," I said. But I
did have a glow stick. I cracked it, and it
started to glow. I put it in a small plastic
bag with some rocks, and I dropped it into
the bag. It sunk to the bottom. It looked
awesome. Gus was looking closely at
the fish.

"Are we going to keep these guys?" he
asked.

"No," I said. "We're going to wait until
it's dark and bring them back down to the
lake." We sat and quietly watched the fish
for a while.

Later, Dawson and the others called in to us.

"Ricky! Gus! It's dinnertime," said Dawson. "C'mon."

"We can't," I said.

"Why not?" asked Dawson.

"We're sick," I said in a croaky voice. "We ate our fish, and we ate too much."

"I don't see any fires," said Dawson. "You're lying."

"We didn't cook them," I said. "We made sushi. Now we're sick."

It was quiet outside the tent. Then I had my best idea of the day. I scooped up the wet crackers and gunk from the low corner of the tent. Gus smiled, because he knew what I was doing. That's how you know you have a best friend, when he can read your mind.

"We're really, really sick!" I said. Then
I started making heaving sounds. Gus
unzipped the bottom of the tent zipper, and
I made a huge barfing sound. I threw the
gunk out of the tent.

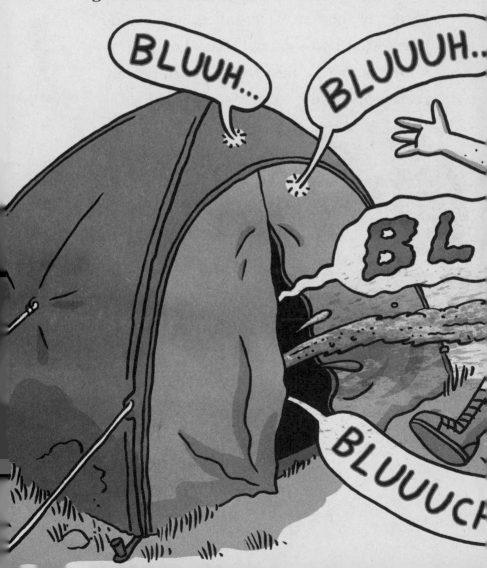

"Ewwwww!" said all the older scouts. "Stay away from us. We don't want to get sick!" They ran off, laughing and talking about how gross we were.

Soon it was dark, and we knew that
the other scouts would all be busy making
a campfire.

I put the backpack on, and we set off
into the woods. It was really dark. We
didn't want anyone to know where we were,
so we couldn't use our flashlights. The
glow stick created an eerie glow from the
backpack. The fish still seemed very happy
and were swimming around.

"Which way?" said Gus.

"Follow me," I said. It was hard to
figure out where to go. We couldn't use any
paths, because we couldn't let anyone see
us. But we knew that the lake was downhill
from camp, so as long as we were walking
down, we'd get there.

We heard a loud snap in the dark woods. Then another. Then there was a thud of some kind. Something big fell.

"That sounds like a bear," I said. "It probably smells the fish."

"Aren't we supposed to back away if a bear sees us?" asked Gus.

"Yeah, we are," I said. We stood still for a moment. Then we heard some fast snapping sounds coming from the other direction.

"What's that?" asked Gus.

"Could be a wolf," I whispered.

"Should we run?" asked Gus.

"YES!" I screamed.

We took off. I could feel the water splashing from the backpack. I jumped over a log, and a fish flew out of the top and hit Gus in the face!

FWOP!

"Ahhhhh!" cried Gus. "It's attacking me!" Luckily it fell into his hands, and he quickly tossed it back into the pack. I ran past a tree, and the pack got caught. A branch went right through the hole and into the plastic bag. Water started pouring out!

"It's leaking!" I screamed.

"Run! Run!" shouted Gus.

We tore through the woods until we could see the lake. I took the pack from my back and tried to carry it with my hand over the hole. I was getting soaked, and I could see the water level going down. We came out of the woods onto the dock, and I dove. The backpack went flying into the lake along with the fish and the glow stick.

We looked down into the water and
could see the fish swimming happily in all
directions. The glow stick lit the water as
we watched them swim away. We pulled
out the pack and other junk. That's when
you came down the path.

"I see," said Scoutmaster Dave.
"I really wish you hadn't run off like this.
It's dangerous in the woods at night."

Ricky and Gus looked upset. "We're
sorry," they said.

"But you two did a noble thing," said the scoutmaster. "You did what you felt was right, and that's how a scout should act."

"Thanks," said Ricky. "But I guess we won't get our fishing badges because we didn't eat the fish, right?"

"Ewww. No," said Scoutmaster Dave. "You caught the fish. You'll get the badge."

Just then, there was another series of quick crashes in the woods, and a few scouts came running onto the dock. Dawson was one of them. They all had buckets with them.

"What are you doing here?" asked the scoutmaster.

Dawson looked embarrassed. "We were coming down to throw our fish back in the water," he said. "We couldn't kill and eat them."

"But why were you running?" asked the scoutmaster.

"I think we heard a bear!" said Dawson.

"Or maybe a wolf!" said Ricky.

They all heard another noise. They became silent and looked into the woods. Ricky, Gus, and the others could hear more rustling.

"There's something in there," whispered the scoutmaster.

There was still a lot of honking on the bridge, but none of the vehicles were moving. Ricky and the man kept talking.

"But why did you hit my car with a belt?" asked the man.

"I'm getting to that," said Ricky. . . .

I looked at the mystery sock, and I slowly reached into it. I took out a crushed piece of sushi and ate it really fast!

"He's eating sock sushi!" said Stew. All the kids laughed and groaned. A piece of floppy baloney was handed to me. It looked pretty normal.

"Big deal!" I said. "It's a slice of baloney!"

IT WAS IN JOHNSON'S ARMPIT!

Michelle was laughing now. "Eww!" she said. "Don't eat it, Ricky! You won! You won!"

I looked at Michelle and reminded her of the rules. "I have to eat whatever is given to me, or I lose!"

I gobbled it down, and everyone on the bus was laughing and screaming and getting grossed out! The teacher stood up and looked back at us, and we all quieted down.

Then everyone started whispering. I could see that all the other kids were up to something. Some bent over and reached under their seats.

A few minutes later, there was a murmur on the bus, and all the kids were looking at me again. Someone handed something to Stew and whispered. Stew handed it to me.

"Gum blob from under the bus seats," whispered Stew. Kids were whisper-chanting, "Eat it! Eat it! Eat it!"

I held the glob of bus seat gum in my hand close to my mouth.

"Ricky! Don't!" whispered Michelle. She was giggling. I could tell she really wanted me to eat it. I've eaten some gross crud before, but this was gonna be the grossest thing ever. But I had to win!

I opened my mouth and brought the gooey, sticky, fuzzy glob to my lips. All of a sudden, the bus jerked forward and into a center lane. I fell back in my seat, and the glob of bus gum went out the window.

"He's cheating!" cried a kid.
"If he doesn't eat it, he loses!"
screamed another. "You lose, Ricky!"

I looked out the bus window and saw
the glob of gum sitting on the roof of a car.
I tried to reach it, but it was way too far.

I knew I had to get that gum back!
I had never lost a game of Garbage Mouth.
I took my belt off really fast.
   "Does anyone have a fork?" I asked.
   Someone gave me a plastic fork.
I pulled my shoelace out of my shoe
(I really should just carry extras) and tied
the fork to the end of the belt.

The traffic had stopped moving again, and the gum car was right next to us.

I hung out the window with my fork-on-a-belt and started twirling it. Then, after it was going fast enough, I aimed it at the gum and whipped it hard. I stabbed the gum on the first try!

"Bull's-eye!" I said.

THUK!

The car moved forward, but we didn't. The gum was stuck on the roof. The belt got really tight. I leaned out the window as far as I could, but the shoelace broke and the fork stayed in the gum. The belt came flying at me and knocked me in the face so hard that I fell back into the bus, across Stew, and into the aisle.

OOF!

THUD!

I jumped up fast and got to the window and tried again to hit the gum with the belt, hoping I could get it back. That's when you stuck your head out the window.

The man looked at Ricky like he was crazy. "You really ate all that gross stuff?" he asked. The kids were looking out the bus windows now.

"Yeah," said Ricky.

The man turned his head and looked at the roof of his car. He reached up and grabbed the bus seat gum glob.

"What happens if someone else eats something that you don't eat?" asked the man.

"Then they win Garbage Mouth, and I lose," said Ricky.

He put the gum in his mouth and
chewed it. Then the traffic opened up, and
he sped away.

Ricky and the kids all sat back down
in the bus. Everyone was laughing hard,
especially Michelle. The bus started moving
again and was soon traveling at full speed.

"Hey!" said Stew. "We're off the bridge."

Michelle looked out the window. "Wow," she said. "Thanks, Ricky."

"No problem," said Ricky.

Then she leaned over the seat and did the most disgusting, gross, horrible thing ever. She gave Ricky a quick kiss on the cheek.